From: JESUS
To: SANTA CLAUS

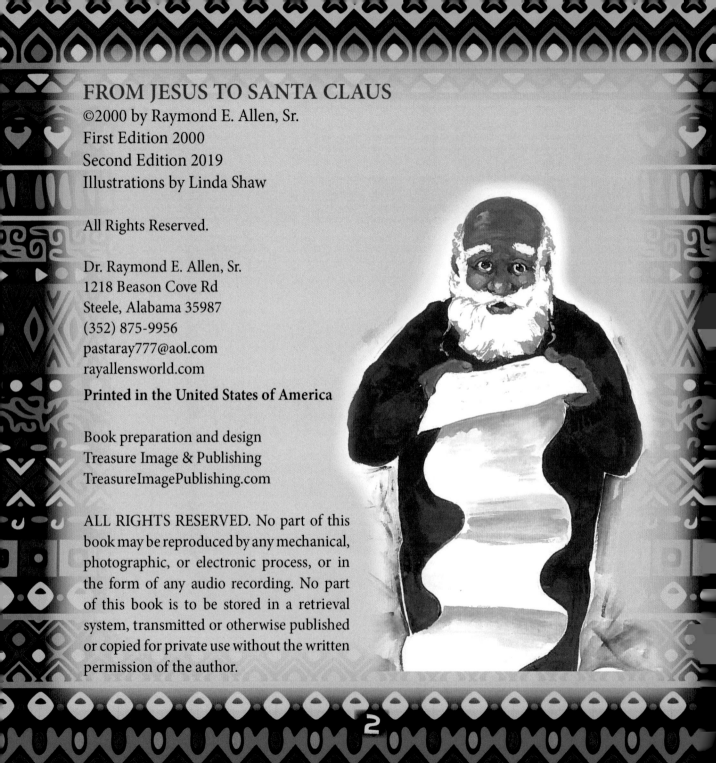

# FROM JESUS TO SANTA CLAUS

©2000 by Raymond E. Allen, Sr.
First Edition 2000
Second Edition 2019
Illustrations by Linda Shaw

Dr. Raymond E. Allen, Sr.
1218 Beason Cove Rd
Steele, Alabama 35987
(352) 875-9956
pastaray777@aol.com
rayallensworld.com

**Printed in the United States of America**

Book preparation and design
Treasure Image & Publishing
TreasureImagePublishing.com

# DEDICATION

First of all I want to give praise and honor to Father God and my Lord and savior Jesus Christ, who by the inspiration of the Holy Spirit gave me this story.

I also dedicate it to my late wife Alma Jean Coleman Allen for being the greatest wife and mother ever, you will never be forgotten.

To all my beautiful children,The A-Team, Raenell, Raymond Jr, Raina, Raquel, Reba, Ryan, and Rashawnda. I love you very much.

To all 26 of my beautiful grandchildren: Papa loves you forever and always.

Special thanks to my daughter and son. Raquel and Bruce Smith for paying for this book to be born, Love you.

Special thanks to Tyrell and Brittany Scott for all your love and support, love you and you guys rock.

And last but not least, I want to thank Lourdes Perez Chaney (Dez) for her constant love and support, never forget how absolutely amazing you are.

# Now if there were a Santa Claus, can you imagine this?

Out of all the millions and millions of names, he saw the name "Jesus" on his list.

Aiden
Alaya
Amarion
Arianna
Ava
Carrie'onna
Christian
Darias
Diontre
Elijah
Harmony
Imani
Isaac

Jaeshawn
Jamiea
Jesus
Joshua
Josiah
Ka'Ray
Kashmir
LeBron
Macey
Marcus Jr.
Mariell
Mercy
Micah

Mira
Nakia
Nakih
Rameal
Raymond III
Reiko
Re'Muan
Revin
Savali
Seaira
Shaelley
Sim'waan
Tariah
Victoria

Then rubbing his eyes,
he checked

once again, not

concerned about

naughty or nice,

But the name was still there and was written in red, and you know the name seemed to have life.

Santa jumped to his feet and ran as fast as he could to the room where he kept all the mail,

Because every name that was on his list sent a letter to him without fail.

Then, searching through the tons of mail... yes, searching high and searching low...

There in the midst of all the mail there was a letter all aglow!

So he picked it up
quickly and
turned it
around slow.

# Was this letter from Jesus?

He just had to know.

# YES!

"From Jesus to Santa" was written in red. He opened it quickly to see what it said.

From:
Jesus

To:
Santa

He put on his glasses, then lowered his head, and this is how the letter read:

Dear Nicholas,
I love you!
Yes, it's really really
Me, and I just want
to let you know that
I have set you free.

Yes, I've seen your true heart every year
in all the gifts you gave. But only my gift
upon the tree can cause man to be saved.

On your list you have been checking who's
been naughty and who's been nice.

But know that it is I, the
Lord, who has paid the
price.

Through all the Christmas years,
Nicholas, you've been faithful
and true blue. That's why this
Christmas I have a gift especially for you.

I hung upon a lonely tree, shed my blood,
and died. When the third day came, I rose
again and my Father glorified.

I saw you there with all
mankind while I
was on that tree.

So Santa friend,
to you I give the
gift of all of ME!

Love, Jesus

Santa's heart was touched that day. He fell on his knees and began to pray.

Then both his hands he began to wave, and wouldn't you know it...
SANTA CLAUS GOT SAVED!

FROM. Santa
TO: You

You've seen what God has done for me
And now I'm in his plan
You've seen how Jesus touched my heart
You've seen me wave my hands

The one who came into my heart
Can also set you free.
So, dear friend, whether young or old
Please bow your head with me.

"Dear Jesus, please come into my heart
I call on you today.
Forgive me, Lord, for all my sins
and wash them all away.

No matter whether Christmas day
I know I'm on your list
Today I'm giving you my heart
Yes, it's my special gift.

Thank you, Lord, for saving me,
Now I'm part of your great plan
'Cause I've prayed the blessed prayer of faith."

Santa said, "Ho! Ho! Ho! Amen!"

34

Made in the USA
Monee, IL
20 October 2022

16259311R00021